I0624622

Other Works by the Author:

the Everything Under novels
Sin Gorge
Jennyripper
The Never-Time Girl

"The World" Children's Novels
Beyond the Grass Ocean
The Nightly Train

Collections
Strange Symphonics: Short Stories for the Long World

Tales of Pon-Chai the Thiefkiller
The Virtuous
The Starling's Worth
A Dream of Jadeite

The Polyphase-Powered Man

Copyright © 2017 by Ron Horsley/Everything Under Press

Cover & Illustrations by Ron Horsley

ISBN-13: 978-0-9903910-3-6
ISBN-10: 0-9903910-3-5

www.midnightersclub.com

Printed in U.S.A

the Polyphase-Powered Man

written by Ron Horsley

For Jerry Williamson, a real irregular type. And Gary Braunbeck, my literary father.

For Bill Nolan, and the soul of Dashiell Hammett.

For my grandfather, Ron the First, the biggest fan of this story ever since the first draft.

And for Pretty, as everything always is.

"The scientists of today think deeply instead of clearly. One must be sane to think clearly, but one can think deeply and be quite insane."

—Nikola Tesla

FILE STORE DES. TES-CROS/1943/NY/USOAP-FBIJ
United States Office of Alien Property
DATE OF RECEIPT: 01/09/1943
DATE OF ARCHIVE: 03/15/1943
Clearance Recorded: John G. Trump (Dr.), Ph.D.
                                   Thomas Braun (OAP Off.#23-489D)

FOIA Request Clear: 11/15/2015,
                                 #013-221B-OH/NY, HORSLEY III, R.J.

NOT TO BE REPRODUCED WITHOUT PERMISSION OF THE U.S. OAP OR DESIGNATE JOINT OFFICE UNDER PENALTY OF BREACH OF NATIONAL SECURITY (USOAP ORD. 800.13 SUB 14/ PAR 3)

January 14th, 1941

I have not often wanted to write of anything personal, or any outright face-to-face experiences. One's work is the most important chronicle that any man can leave to others if they wish to truly know about him and what his life was worth. Not the day-to-day mess of sleeping, eating and having to walk around with the rest of the lost world.

But I feel a need to write this particular experience down while I still have sufficient wit and memory of all of its details to do so. And while my personal notes, separate from my professional ones, are still not constantly sniffed at and fingered by bumbling Patent officers. They treat any formula on a dinner napkin worth the level of a diary of da Vinci, the way you can almost hear their nostrils flare and sniff.

I may be thought of now as a doddering and fantasy-addled old tinkerer (then of course, if I am so useless and past my time why do they still want to come by to peek in at my scribbles?). But I can tell you with this bit of writing of a time when another man's mind made my own seem a child's in comparison.

Perhaps it might give some idea to my industrial successors what it means to have real respect for one's equals.

And especially for one's betters.

I was still sitting in the small ad hoc office within the main Electricities Building when Westinghouse brought the investigator in to see me.

It was April 28th of 1893, and I was barely days from being completely ruined before the world stage. You may appreciate then why I was seated, and why I had not moved for the better part of the morning since I'd been brought in on the discovery.

And here now, just after the lunch-hour while the workmen were still wandering about outside, being necessarily diverted from the main floor and the public revelation of the theft, came Westinghouse with his "private investigator." I found him as cold and dislikable a man as I had met. And I had met many men I'd found reason to dislike since coming to America.

"Mr. Sheldon Howard." Westinghouse introduced him, leading the taller man by a hand lightly resting on one knobbed shoulder. "I'd like you to meet Nikki Tesla, the project head and inventor of the generators, amongst other things at this exhibit." He swept his other hand towards me, even as some unseen assistant was already closing the door on the office. In the tight space of the room, already a third filled with a desk, chair and myself, it was practically a closet with the three of us there.

I wanted to admonish Westinghouse. I hate when someone is lazy with my mother-given name. But Westinghouse only tolerated me because of my facility with the machines he purchased. I knew as of that morning that I was not indispensable to him. He could hire a thousand electrical engineers after me, and he'd paid for the patent rights after all.

I didn't have to be any sort of alienist to know that it didn't make Westinghouse feel any better that my compatriot Mr. Clemens often called him *"The soul of Reason…if Reason were a drunkard technologist,"* or that I'd repeated that comment at one of Westinghouse's summer-house parties last July. He was already getting enough colorful remarks made at his expense the closer that the launch day of the exhibit loomed.

Better to be the humor than the humored, I decided. I shook myself awake and stood to greet them. I held out a hand and tried to not show it was an effort. "Mr. Howard."

As quickly as my hand was grasped, it was released after a single hard pump of wrists. Howard's face was tight, a visible sign that he had as much aversion to the ridiculous tradition of shaking hands as I did. As the grip released, though, I saw a faint flash at the man's inner wrist. Before the hand returned to its side and blocked the view, I could see clearly it was no sort of tattoo, but rather a splotch of skin mottled with the slightly dark, aged blushes of old chemical damage. As if the man had long worked with a lab…and materials some of which were caustic in nature, hence the discolored skin.

"Mr. Howard is an investigator for Scotland Yard. He's considered one of the best to serve on this case, at my personal request."

"I was already in New York," Howard replied. "It was little trouble to make Chicago a diversion for a time." His British accent was familiar as a smell of old pipe tobacco or the cool of a favored mug handle's porcelain; I had heard it in so many variations on my travel by steamship to America, several years before. "I would be interested to see the scene of the crime straight away, please.

I cast a quick glance at Westinghouse, who gave a curt nod indicating it was to be done.

"This way, then." I hoped my agitation was as clear in my voice as this stranger's brusqueness had been in his. I managed to move around them and open the door, sweeping a hand to indicate the way towards the presentation floor.

How could I describe the man that followed me, lit by the glow of the emergency gas-lamps that had been brought in and strung up by their hoses that gray and overcast afternoon?

He was a man best suited to serving as an artist's model. Perhaps a sculptor, if a sculptor were looking for a model to represent Arrogance like a virtue akin to a Michelangelo, or a Botticelli.

There was the heroic about him. He had strong shoulders; his arms, though gangling at his sides, moved with a grace that was reminiscent of a pair of well-oiled tension-brads in motion as they stirred a dynamo to life. He was thin-faced, like scarecrows I had seen on long train-rides from New York to Chicago. Nature had made his nose large, his chin long, as if to accommodate more of what was stuffed inside to fill them. His lips were nonexistent. There were deep worry-lines to the sides of his crow's-beak nose.

He wore a strangely foreign cut of longcoat: a cloak more than coat, except that it buttoned shut instead of being allowed to flap at his back. All brown cloth and herringbone tweed, with his hair black save for some faint silver at the temples. The only accents of light to him were his bright, roving eyes. Beyond any thoughts of statues and scarecrows, when I glanced back at his features so thrust forward, the eyes rolling and almost feeding on everything in sight, I thought more of some sort of monstrous lighthouse. Capable of striding the coasts and beaming down on every small crack and stone. He had overtaken me and walked alongside me, as if he didn't need any direction even in a building he had never set foot in before today.

"I hope you can resolve this issue quickly." Westinghouse was blustering to cover his embarrassment as he followed behind. "These generators were supposed to be the flagship of my exhibit when the Exposition opens in a few days." A huff of breath. If Howard was expected to say something in agreement or acknowledgment, Westinghouse was defeated. "If we have no power source, then I have no investment, you see. And well...I don't have to draw you a picture of what this country...never mind my personal fortune...may well look like if my generators aren't seen for the innovation this country needs."

I kept looking ahead, as if I were a pony pulling a dog-cart, low-hung head and indifference in every step.

'My' generators. As if to suggest that Westinghouse, all silk ascots and diamond tie-pins, had so much as coiled a single induction line, or soldered a single weld.

Howard nodded, not looking at Westinghouse but at the floor as we walked. "Indeed," he remarked. His word sounded as offhand as if he'd let it drop, a discarded handkerchief he no longer had use for.

Westinghouse, flustered, fell silent. It was clear that Mr. Howard wasn't interested in sales pitches of grief and financial loss. Neither was I, to be frank. Men like George Westinghouse were great means to the ends of advance, but in themselves were perhaps more the stones in the river that help define its course through obstructing its flow rather than facilitating any great surge forward.

"None of the men working here were aware of any intrusion until we came in this morning," I said, accompanying Howard around the double rows of clean-concrete rectangles. Twelve feet by fifteen feet apiece, they were where the generators had been mounted by industrial steel bolts to the concrete.

"I could not be here at the delivery of the devices to the building earlier this week," I explained. "I'm at an important stage of sorting out some problems with a new conductor coil and had to remain at the Westinghouse main laboratory a few days more. I had trusted that the machines would be set up according to my instructions. I was only arriving last night for the last few days' of preparation and testing before the opening. I arrived in Chicago and barely spent more than an hour last night after I got off the train, walking and making a general inspection of the machines."

I pointed to a number of the rectangles' outer lines. "It looks like the bolt-heads were cut, and the generators removed from them."

"A good guess," Howard said, not looking at me but at the one-inch-diameter metal pegs in the borders of the rectangles. He came to a stop so quickly that I had taken a few steps beyond him before realizing it, and turned to step back towards him as Howard lowered himself to his haunches, like a tracker assessing a fresh trail in the woods. "But an altogether wrong one. Where are the heads of the bolts, then?"

I looked around. It was true. The technicians had been ordered not to sweep or move anything until Westinghouse approved it. There had subsequently been police guard to keep onlookers and laborers from just wandering around the Westinghouse Exhibit space inside the Electricities Building of the Exposition.

"Taken with them?"

Howard shook his head.

"The bolts were severed at the heads by a powerful acid, delicately applied." Howard pointed to the smoothness of the tops of the bolts. "Bolt-shears would have left angular, pinched ends, and in some of them outright tears in the metal. But instead, these all have uniformly smooth, almost glass-like, surfaces, all even and without angle. Further..." He stepped back from the clean rectangle's border, indicating with a crisp tap of his shoe-tip on the floor, where there was a scattering of light, pocked dots all around the square edge of clean concrete. "...These drops show where that same acid was spilled during its use. Not so much as to be obvious, but enough that it left definite signs behind, after the deed was done."

"An excellent belief," I snapped. "But that is just one possibility."

"One supported by the testimonies of your employees," Howard said, unruffled. He bent over, plucking a headless bolt from its housing, tossing it to me like it was nothing more than an egg or a sports ball. "Look at the evidence up close, if you'd care to."

I looked at the bolt. Turned it over in my hands. Ran my fingertips over the severed head. I conceded to it by putting it in my coat pocket, referring to it no further.

"To do as you suggest, going one at a time with bolt cutters that require significant time and pressure to make work even under ideal circumstances, would take a crew twice that of your own some hours to complete. You, yourself, left this exhibit around eleven in the evening and returned, bright and early, the following morning at six, did you not?"

"How would you know that it was eleven?"

"I was on the first express from Philadelphia, connecting from New York, that ran at six this morning. One of the conductors was kind enough to provide me with a copy of yesterday's timetables. The only remaining train on last night's express runs on the same route would have arrived no earlier than nine, or half-past with luggage delays. You arrived here right after disembarking and spent the better part of an hour, according to your account. The new train station is only but a handful of blocks from this site, so you could not have been held up that long between arrival and inspection. As to when you came in this morning, I've already been briefed on that by Mr. Westinghouse while on the ride here today."

"Yes. Well it means that whoever took the generators couldn't have had very long to do the job."

"Seven hours." Howard nodded to himself. His brow curved down, his eyes clouding with some internal calculation. "Seven hours to get into the building, free the generators, and somehow remove them from this place without anyone seeing or suspecting anything was wrong."

"That's not entirely true."

Westinghouse had released himself from the clutch of the assistants momentarily, and was standing a few feet away watching us. His voice was low and punctuated by a clearing of his throat as he finished.

Howard arched an eyebrow. "How so?"

"It is true that no one suspected anything. But there would have been noise, motion." He flapped a hand indicating the air around us. "I've been here the better part of this week making sure the promotions are set up and seeing to various arrangements with the city council, and it has been a madhouse over every square inch of the grounds, not just this building. With the Exposition's Opening Day coming up a few days from now, there's already a lot of around-the-clock building and hauling." His hand spidered up to rub at his ascot with a nervous obliviousness. "It is altogether likely that the thieves simply blended into the background as soon as they completed the robbery."

"They probably just loaded the generators there," I pointed at the far end of the Electricities Building, where two large barn-style double doors were now closed. "And proceeded as if they were another delivery of building materials."

"Good," Howard mused. "That clears up part of the mystery, that of how they were able to get away with it." Howard turned to Westinghouse. "Did you not post guards on the site?"

Westinghouse cleared his throat again. The fingers fumbled at the ascot as if he were trying to unravel it by hand, thread by thread.

I knew why but couldn't say anything. I'd asked that he do just the very thing, but he'd cited that too much money and time was wasted with the exhibit already, not even having opened successfully yet. It wasn't worth it to *call up the Pinkerton Agency and have paid thugs lounging around on my payroll,* his exact words.

Howard had immediately hit on a sensitive nerve of the issue that had been a thorn between Westinghouse and I since the discovery of the theft.

I could see the twist in my backer's lips and changed the subject before Westinghouse answered. "How did they get in at all?"

"Easily enough," Howard said. To illustrate, he merely pointed an index finger skywards. Up at the skylight of glass and steel arches.

There was a large, precision-cut shadow, a circle three feet in diameter, lighter than the rest of the panes. A hole, cut into the glass by someone (or someones) who had then lowered down from the skylight into the unattended exhibit.

"I take it you hadn't noticed because there's been no rain the last few days," Howard said. "Now, if you wouldn't mind, Mr. Tesla, I'm unfamiliar with the layout of the Exposition, so I'd like to ask if we could take a walk together. To clear the air, perhaps even let these gentlemen—" he nodded to the technicians and the other exhibit-tenders mumbling around, hands in pockets, "—finish their tasks."

"Certainly, Mr. Howard." I spoke through nearly-clenched teeth. I strode out quickly, not bothering to see if he followed as I headed to the massive wing doors at the nearest end of the building. Westinghouse was quickly swallowed by his ever-hungry entourage of questioners and order-conveyors.

We walked out of the Electricities Building, onto the promenade walkway that bordered the marble-rimmed pool that was the centerpiece for the Exposition.

Chicago was balmy and cool; reminiscent of summer nights I'd enjoyed as a boy in Croatia. There was still something of the oily smoke-smell coming off the lake's direction, you couldn't fully escape it no matter where you might try to go within city limits. But it almost felt as though the Exposition, in all its shining and glistening amazement waiting to be unleashed on the world, balked even the winds from bringing too harsh a stink off the waterways and their ships, or the city streets that cloistered like fingers round the slaughterhouse district and made the city reek of copper and blood, iron and rot. This was the City of Tomorrow, we were announcing to the world. And in Tomorrow, there would be little need for such corruption as those old ways offered.

Howard fell in step beside me, shortening his long-legged pace to my own. Those lighthouse eyes were on everything: tracking the few evening laborers who passed us by, carrying buckets and lengths of lumber...a small cluster of starlings that flew overhead...the lap of small waves in the marble pool. There was a constant sound of hammering, thumping and hollers from one workman to another like a strange, broken song. Buildings were still being hastily finished and exhibits elsewhere constructed in time for the Opening Day.

We made a casual circuit of the pool, passing underneath Mistress Columbia's stern regard, then a lazy gait towards the North Canal that ran off from the main pool alongside the Electricities Building.

"Forgive my suggesting as much, sir," Howard kept a level face while he spoke; his voice was filled with cold acid. "You don't seem to really care about the theft of the generators Mr. Westinghouse has so heavily invested in."

I sucked in a gasp, stopping in half-step. Howard stopped beside me. How dare he—?

How can I even begin to explain to those of you who weren't there, what an utter shock and monument the World's Exposition was, the entire sweep of the Columbia Exhibit?

Could I even capture a tenth of the meaning behind such sights as the Midway? When I first laid eyes on the Court of Honor, the broad and shallow mall of water and white marble that terminated at one end with massive arched bridges and at the other a vibrant, arms-held-high statue of Lady Victory, Columbia herself, atop her Ship of Progress, oars splayed out along its sides like eagle wings? The whole thing, even to a man who was familiar with the largesse and grandeur of my home country and its surrounding castle villages, was astounding in its scope. I was standing amidst it with my exhibit and still found it hard to believe it was almost all constructed in only twenty-odd months, on a scrap of muddy mire beside the lake.

The only thing I could really say was horrid to me was the sight of the Court of Honor at night, when I'd left the Electricities Building to head back to the hotel for a short night's sleep before returning to supervise the final assembly of the exhibit.

Lit by ten thousand strung electric lights, powered by an already-obsolete Allis generator buried under steam and smoke inside the Electricities Building at the far end from the Westinghouse AC displays.

The Court of Honor: the limestone-paved, street-lamped walkway and terrace that surrounded the pool and statues...as the twilight deepened into a violet nightfall...the bulb filaments would flicker, the conduit joists would give the faintest of sputters as sparkling power cracked through them, whip-sharp and fast as thought...then the bulbs would seem to take a breath and as one would flare into brilliant life, just as dusk ultimately surrendered to the black of night.

Lights outlined the bridges, the edge of the basin, the dais of the statue, the facades of the buildings that lined along the gallery-sidewalks of it all. Ten thousand lights, culminating in their great Prodigal. A tower eighty-two feet in height, dripping with electric lights with a magnesium-white intensity.

All the bulbs...every strut in the grand Tower...

...all of it designed by that Direct Current bastard.

The one they teach today in school as "the Father of the Light Bulb."

A beautiful sight...one that I ached in loving. Oh, there was rage in that love.

I wanted to grab any of the laborers who were hoisting metal or assembling plaster-cast *fleur-de-lis* fronts for the Palace of Fine Arts as we passed it...I wanted to grab them, whirl them around, show them the lights as they gleamed like a man-made constellation of the heavens and say *Here, see? I did this! Thomas couldn't have put so much as a wire to a spark, if I hadn't shown him the principle of vacuum-gas formation and electrified carbon wire! Look! Look, damn you!*

And someone had stolen that. They hadn't even had the dignity to try and buy it from me, like Edison or Westinghouse had.

Direct Current was an imbecilic dream compared to my alternating energy. But Edison was never a true scientist, never a man who fell in love with the lightning and waves as I did. And Westinghouse never dared so much as set foot in a laboratory, anymore.

But at their worst, *they* had never just blithely come along and carried away all that I had slaved on, like stealing a sweet from a child on the street and leaving it crying, weeping behind them. *They* were buyers and manipulators, schemers and in many ways thieves of the world in their own right. But they came with the chequebook and the lawyers; they didn't steal away in the dead of night and leave the broken bolts and holes of my work, stolen as surely as teeth from my skull.

Whoever this thief was, they'd done worse than steal a dream or dash a hope.

All of this went through my mind as I looked at Howard's face.

"No," I said. "I do not take any of this lightly at all, Mr. Howard." My head looked over the green-black expanse that should have been the glittering ocean of the basin waters except for the stormcloud-threatened skies of late afternoon overhead. "And if you ever suggest that I do not care for recovering the fruits of my labors," I added quietly, "you and I will have more than harsh words between us."

Howard nodded. "I suspected as much, Mr. Tesla. And I am relieved that that eliminates, to my satisfaction, yet another of the possible explanations for this crime."

"You seem to have a list of things you wish to consider."

Howard began walking briskly, away from the Court's limestone walkways, back towards the Electricities Building. "I do, indeed, Mr. Tesla. I must go through a list in all cases, eliminating all that which can be a source of the act...and what is left, I take as the truth."

I jogged after him. "Why are we going back to the generator house?"

"Because while we took this brief walk," Howard called back, "the police bumblers and interfering on-lookers are no doubt fully removed from the scene. Now we can investigate the site in earnest."

****

Howard went through the space with a slower, more thorough motion than he'd done previously. He moved as a man who knew where everything belonged, who never needed a map, no matter where in the world he might go. I was beginning to understand the methodology of the man behind the attitude of cold detachment. He was not unfriendly, merely unequaled.

I could respect...empathize with such a position. I had been fired from several labs for such a thing. Better to dig ditches in quiet than work anywhere where my thoughts were not considered my own.

"It is merely a question of finding what others have missed." He scuffed a shoetip over those dissolved spots of acid-damaged floor.

Two of my technicians remained, one of them reading a paper while the other swept the floor, trying to keep busy. Without a single generator to tend to, they were little more than night watchmen, watching nothing at all.

While Howard searched, I looked around the floor as well. For what, I had no idea. So of course, with no idea of what to look for, I found it.

"Has anyone noticed this?" I asked, walking to the center of one of the clean-floor rectangles, picking up the dingy square of paper I'd spied.

"What?" Howard turned around sharply; there was genuine terror in that gesture, as if the very suggestion that he'd possibly overlooked something was anathema to him. "What do you refer to?" He quickly regained his calm.

"This card," I said, holding up the square.

One of the technicians, MacAbee, shrugged. "We figured it was one of your cue-marks from before the machines were brought in, sir."

I shook my head. "No, I didn't use cards." To Howard, I explained: "Per my instructions on the exhibit floorplans, the technicians used chalk-lines to indicate to the workmen where to place the generators. This is a handwritten card, left in the middle of the floor after the generators were gone. This certainly wasn't here before they were installed."

Ron Horsley

Howard pointed to the card in my grasp. "Your reasoning may not entirely fit the solution, but your conclusion is nonetheless right. I note that as you release the card, it bows slightly in the middle, as often occurs with stationery paper stored in a large packet. Had it been underneath the generators, no doubt it would have long since had any bend or warp to its pulp crushed flat out of it. Let's adjourn to the workroom," Howard spoke with a very businessman-like quickness. "I would like to more carefully examine that item, Mr. Tesla, if you'd bring it with you."

****

Westinghouse had remained even after he'd gotten rid of the newspaper-men and directed the police to tighten their cordon. He was in the small office, out of the light of skylights. A gaslit lamp brought a warm shine to the tiny space. The only sound was his whuffling breaths of cigar smoke while he sat at the desk, and the click-tack of my timing clock, used to make sure the priming of the generators was consistent, hanging on the far wall from the door.

Howard preceded me into the room, the card carried between my fingers like a glass slide.

I had eyed the writing on it while carrying it to the room. The card was worded in a manner I was unfamiliar with. Much of my English has come by way of the heavily-colloquial American version of that tongue, bolstered by my own hours of self-taught reading and exercise in the language. I suppose it has been to my advantage. I am less caught off-guard like many immigrants by the turns of American slang. Westinghouse used them endlessly.

The text was crisply written, in a hand that reminded me of a pharmacist's. Lilting, lightening the ink at the ends of the delicate script. But the impression of the dark vowels and beginning capitalization, almost burned into the paper by the pressure that had been applied, made me think this was the hand of a person who was intelligent, cultured...but utterly enraged.

> "*To Mssr. Westinghouse* [it read], **upon the Discovery of Your Loss:**
>
> *I thank you for the use of your generators, and have no doubts as to the inconvenience I have unavoidably caused*

20

you and your company.

I cannot promise you, with any fealty to the truth, that your generators will not be put to what could be construed as a selfish purpose. However, I bear you no direct ill-will, and as long as you remain non-pursuant to the return of what is now exclusively my property, that position will remain similarly unchanged.

I am not, however, a man who will take to being incommoded by any attempts at recovery for your devices. I hope you will seek out your own better ends, and take heed to my warning."

The card was unsigned.

I read this the first time with utter perplexity. On a second pass I was bothered by the length of the letter. It was not so much that a card had been left at all. A playful ingenuity and ego more than any real desire to warn us away from trying to recover the generators. It was the way in which it avoided the concept entirely.

It did not say simply "don't try to follow us" like I had seen in so many of the Western-Adventure serial publications I read on the occasional day of rest from my work. It went to great lengths to be careful, clear yet clouded at the same instant.

Westinghouse reached for it, read it, and then handed it back to me with that same burnished scowl on his face. For once, the speechmaker was at a loss for words.

I handed it to Mr. Howard, who didn't bother with any delicacy in clasping it between his fingers. I was even further shocked by the immediate change it wrought in his face.

Howard took the card in hand, read it with a short flicker of his eyes from left to right down its half-dozen lines, and I saw his features change.

In some of the penny dreadfuls, like many in Europe, it is often sensationalized to "see the blood drain out" of a face. In Howard, this was made true. He lost all vitality in his features. He did not pale, but there seemed a complete drop in all animation to his face. For just a moment, I saw something I had not thought I should see in so austere a man:

The fingers holding the card shook.

Ron Horsley

For just a heartbeat, as if he had suffered one of those static-charge shocks I come across so often in my work. But they did shake, without any attempt to hide or explain them.

"'Incommoded,'" Howard whispered.

"Do you have some idea about what or who we're dealing with?" I asked.

Howard looked at the card again. I saw something on his face that looked nervous. But yet I could swear that when the man began speaking, tapping the card against his other hand the whole while, the timbre of his tone was almost *pleased*.

"His career has been an extraordinary one," Howard spoke like a mechanical thing. "He is a man of good birth and excellent education. Endowed by nature with a phenomenal mathematical faculty." He spoke slowly, deliberately choosing his words with a care. "A criminal strain runs in his blood, which, instead of being modified, is increased and rendered infinitely more dangerous by his extraordinary mental powers."

"Who the hell are you talking about, man?" Westinghouse demanded, an impatient wave of his cigar-laden hand for emphasis.

"Someone I thought I had dealt with some time ago, Mr. Westinghouse." Howard slowly blinked, like waking from a heavy sleep. "Someone who is, in the end, the very first person I should have suspected of all this...had I not had the impression that he was already dead."

I broke composure. "Who?"

Howard took in a breath.

"None other than Professor Moriarty, late of London, England." A shiver ran across his chest, out to his shoulders. "A mastermind of engineering and strategies like none of this age I've ever seen. With, of course," Howard nodded at me, smiling a thin smirk, "all due respects to your own ingenuity, Mr. Tesla."

"But—"

"I'm sorry, but I suppose it's time to be completely honest with you." Howard's smile was cold; the tone of humor utterly removed from his voice. He straightened to his full height, no longer slouching or trying to efface an air of humility. "I am revealed to you, Mr. Tesla. May I reintroduce myself to you as Sherlock Holmes, also late of London, England."

Holmes idly flicked his wrist, fingers unclasping. The card spun, fluttered, and landed print-side up on the desk.

I swallowed deeply, my eyes going first at Westinghouse, then back to the calm, inexpressive face of the detective.

It was clear that, as the man who had contracted him, Westinghouse had been in the knowing of this fact since the beginning.

I had heard of Sherlock Holmes before coming to America and trying to ridiculously ingratiate myself in the idiot Edison's laboratory-factory. Not a lot was published about him, save the one or two articles that had been written when he'd helped reveal plots or crimes relevant to major political powers.

"How...how is it you know this man so well? Was he a colleague of yours back in England?"

Holmes sighed. "In a sense. You might say, as dearly as I miss and appreciate the company of my old friend Watson, that Professor Moriarty is the only true colleague a man like myself will ever have." He sat down in a nearby chair, seeming to sink his gaunt form to the wood. A hand fluttered skeletally to shade his face, as if a bright electric light had been brought to bear on him. "I had hoped...I had hoped that he had died in our last confrontation. Last? I should have only hoped, foolish as I was, that it was truly the last."

"How-so foolish of you, Holmes?" Westinghouse inquired, taking a long puff on his dwindling tobacco. The reek of it had filled the whitewashed little office. I waved my hand before my face, irritated. A stray scree of light glinted off his tie-pin, and I felt the beginnings of a headache seep into my skull.

"Because I allowed myself a fantasy in place of logic, for perhaps the first time since I endeavored to live as a private man of deduction." Holmes spoke from behind his embarrassment-raised hand. "I allowed myself to believe, not because of any true evidence to support it, that Moriarty had died when we fought. Shortly after he first came to reveal himself to me as my nemesis, there was...an encounter. A fall. We confronted one another and I...I felt an obligation to make certain that I saw to his end. However...I still..." The hand at his face swung down, slamming with a hard thump into the armrest at his side. "*Damnable* fool! I still clung to my own life...I thought I had been so clever, so deft at letting him fall to his own ends while I contrived to avoid the risk altogether...I survived...it was idiocy to think that such as he could not have done so as well. As seemingly impossible as it should have appeared, I should have remembered my own adage, my own fool's advice. Where any man, with will and grim determination to survive may do so, surely a man such as Moriarty would have...damn it all..."

I was puzzled. "I never heard of this."

Holmes did that ineffable flapping of his hand again. "It wouldn't have been publicized. My friend, Inspector Lestrade, was given sufficient evidence by my executor Dr. Watson to pursue the gang that had been under Moriarty's guidance. My part in the drama was down-played deliberately."

Westinghouse nodded. "I had to go through a lot of trouble to find out you really weren't dead, Mr. Holmes. A great deal of trouble and expense. When the generators were taken, I knew enough through my English interests to think of you. I hadn't heard that you were believed dead until it was too late to back out of the search." The cigar, down to its last quarter, was stubbed out in a marble ashtray larger than some of the pestles I used in mixing iron filings. "Your Inspector Lestrade was willing to provide me with your contact information since you were in New York already, and your brother...your brother—"

"Mycroft."

"Yes. Mycroft. Secretariat of your Crown's defense department, as best I could determine. A formidable sibling you have, there." Westinghouse grunted with approval. "At first he insisted he hadn't even seen you, let alone confirmed your survival. It took a bit of hemming and hedging to get him to even surrender and finally agree to the ruse of all this. He provided that I go to the further trouble of falsifying your travel documents, to support this absurd 'Sheldon Howard' identity you've been hiding under, available only at your signature and personal appearance at the agreed location in New York. Not a very convincing name, I might add." Westinghouse sat at his desk, frowning in that perpetual grimace of his.

"On the contrary." Holmes smiled, more to me than to Westinghouse. "Names are an integral key-stone to changing one's identity. To that end, I selected a name phonetically close enough to my own that if someone referred to me by it, I should react to it as naturally and instantly as to my real one." Holmes pursed his lips to expel a tired breath. "Had I selected something more outré, there was a risk that I would never fully settle into that character, and thus my identity might be more quickly compromised. But it is no matter." His eyes bore into me; they reminded me for a second of the bastard Edison--neither men ever apparently lacked for conviction or self-determination. "Can I trust that, aside from those of us in the room, that 'Sheldon Howard' shall remain in Mr. Westinghouse's employment for this case?"

I nodded slowly. "Yes, Mr. Hol—Howard."

Holmes nodded. "Good man. Now...Mr. Tesla, I'm afraid there can be no more hiding or hedging of our respective bets." Holmes steepled his fingers, now much more at ease in his own native mind again. "What sort of power can your alternating-current generators provide, given the near-limitless imagination that such as Moriarty can bring to bear on their application?"

****

It was an hour for me to explain to Holmes the principles of the machine involved. To any layman, even Westinghouse, it would have required more time to go through the processes of alternating current, polyphase dual generators, and all the associated machinery.

But Holmes had an educated mind, as only I could have expected of a man with his reputation. He never asked questions, only allowed me to continue. Every so often I would pause, expecting a question to come up to explain a term or concept. But I would only find those hawk's eyes, probing me, waiting for me to continue.

After the impromptu lecture, I fell silent. Holmes did not choose to fill the silence immediately. I could hear the timing clock hanging on the wall for several minutes.

"If he chooses to," Holmes asked at last, "what sort of effect could he create with the generators?"

"I honestly couldn't say. The power is controlled but still immense... with sufficient oil and tending, the machines were built to be very reliable for long periods. He could power a ship, create lightning from literally the thin air, run an entire factory or even small community with the power... what sort of man is this professor?"

"A man not to be underestimated." It was all Holmes offered. "Now... twelve generators, encompassing a massive amount of space, requiring further space for ventilation...and perhaps some consideration for the noise such huge devices would generate while in use...unless Moriarty cares nothing for who hears him." Holmes's eyes were on the face of the timing clock, hanging on the wall. "Are there any symptoms of the machines while in use? Anything that denotes them specifically from other engines of their scale?"

"Magnetism," I replied. "Same as electrifying any small wire, passing that much current through their housings causes the generators to produce a small but noticeable magnetic field."

"Go on."

"You've already mentioned the noise. Oh, and heat. They'll produce an astounding amount of heat, but...oh, yes...only after they've been in use for a little over twelve hours, if my metallurgical tests have borne out in the real use."

"Have they?"

"I have no reason to think otherwise."

Holmes checked them off on his fingers. "Magnetic field, heat, noise... anything else?"

"They will spark periodically. Not the machines, really, but the magnetic fields around them. I suspect the fields excite nearby air-borne particles. Sometimes to the point of ignition. And..."

I raised a hand to my lips, brushing my mustache.

"Oh God," I uttered.

"What?"

"I forgot about the governors!"

"The current-tending devices you mentioned?"

"Yes! If anything were to happen to any of the governors, then the generator attached to the faulty one would surge. Its current would be unstopped!"

"You explained as much earlier. Are the generators interconnected?"

"If this man has set them up in the same manner they were set up here, then yes. The generators are set up in a relay, each one's governor stepping down their electricity to a usable, semi-direct form. Then that electricity is relayed through the series. It allows us to create great energy, but still manage the flow, and not lose the power over larger distances. With a totally direct-current system, you'd have to have a generator virtually every twenty feet just to power the lights along the basin outside."

"So...if the governor of one of the generators is damaged?"

"Then the resulting voltage would cause a surge through the entire relay. It could theoretically build into the next generator, overriding its governor. And so on...until—"

"Until a gigantic burst of electricity rips free of the series," Holmes finished.

"Exactly. Where that energy goes...who could guess? If this Moriarty were near the lakeside districts...the electricity could seek a better conduit. Water is a massive conductor...I've practiced bouncing short bolts of electricity across the lake near my lab in New York. You can do it like skipping a stone...but a stone eventually succumbs to gravity. Electricity will keep going, losing relatively little charge until it finds a surface conducive to its transmission."

"Which could be a ship," Holmes remarked, eyes returning from the clock's face to mine. "Or hapless bystanders nearby."

"It would be the electric equivalent of a dynamite bomb. But with virtually no limit to how much power could be continually pumped into the process, how much damage could be ultimately struck using it?"

"Then Moriarty will either commit wanton destruction through design...or simple incompetence," Holmes concluded, getting up from his seat. "The course chosen is simple: how much space would he need? A great deal. Is there a place where one can acquire a map of Chicago at this time of evening?"

****

The map was available at the Administration Building, at the heart of the Court of Honor, looking out past Columbia's statue over the basin.

Holmes unfurled it over a long librarian's table in the Architectural Planner's office. I switched on an electric lamp over the table, my eyes bleary with exhaustion but not failing to notice the way the lamp's light kept shuddering. The Allis generators were already antiques, next to my machines. A candle would've been more reliable, I inwardly remarked.

Holmes pored over the map.

"What are you looking for?"

"Logistic probability." His eyes stayed on the map, roving its lines. "We are looking for a locale where Moriarty would realistically be able to keep the generators, and also provide for their installation and use, with relative anonymity."

"It would not take all that much room." I moved to the other side of the table so I could look upon the map as well. "The generators are bulky, but only twelve feet by fifteen in length, and only about ten feet high. They are massive, but not even the size of a small elephant. Provided he was able to get them on a wagon or truck-bearer, like what was used to transport them here from New York...he could take them to any number of places."

"What we are looking for would be an area with specific characteristics. A place with plenty of space for him to work with the generators, in an area where no one would question his purchase of the property or his use of it at odd hours. He may be operating through a false operation as well — an intercessor or lawyer who represents him here in America. I know of at least three he has used in the past, though none of them have been contacted recently."

I scanned the map. Not being familiar with Chicago beyond the boundaries of the Exposition where I'd been planning the floor arrangement of the exhibit for weeks, there wasn't much I could look for. Holmes should not have been any more familiar with Chicago than I, but looked with much more clarity than I seemed able to muster.

"Here." He pointed a bony finger. "A district of warehouse properties, along the..." He read the small print "...the Lakeshore district. If London is any microcosm of the New World's practices, then the warehouse district would be ideally suited. Around-the-clock goings-on that nobody would be in a position to question. The relative proximity of the types of people Moriarty would employ, and the most important factor: space to operate."

"How can you tell it is a warehouse district?" I pulled the map closer to my view. "This is just a map of streets and neighborhoods!"

"Approximate spacing of the streets on the map," he explained, pointing out how the downtown streets, including those of Jackson and Washington Parks where the Exposition was stretched like a massive canvas, were much closer together on the map. In the area Holmes was looking, they had significantly more space amongst them, indicating that there were larger plots of land. "Larger areas suggest larger structures using the land. And that close to Lake Michigan, I have to make the logical assumption that that is where a major shipping, and thus warehouse, district would lie. Moriarty is nothing if not a creature of atmosphere. His character is an index of his behaviors, no man can escape that truth."

"Is there not some risk that your Moriarty will have...allies?"

"You are referring, no doubt, to the fact that to have accomplished the theft, Moriarty would have to have employed quite a few men, most likely men of the unsavory type. A valid concern, but I ultimately believe a baseless one."

"Why?"

"Because...Moriarty likes to work alone in the final summation of any plot he devises. True, he would have men to perform the theft, to set up the equipment for his inspection, much as you have your technicians here under your supervision...mayhap he even attended the theft and installations himself, overseeing their labors. Yet like any spider at the heart of a web, Moriarty cannot trust catspaws and servants with too much of any great plan, and spiders do not stalk in packs as the wild cats do. Most likely he would have had them deliver the generators to his safekeeping, and discharged them to be called back at such time as he could need them later. Moriarty is not a man who likes company in his personal ruminations. No doubt wherever the generators are, Moriarty is working with them by himself."

"That would be difficult." I frowned. "It takes a minimum of three men to affect maintenance on the generators. Even I have only been able to maintain them alone for an hour or two, when running a trial on one."

"Moriarty is capable to taking on the work himself, if it is possible at all."

"How is it you know this man so well, if you only knew him a short while?"

"*What man may know another, if not to better know himself?*" Holmes said. My face must have given away my ignorance. "Diogenes. Now...we must continue with the chase."

"Shouldn't we contact Mr. Westinghouse?"

"Your trepidation is appreciated, but not appropriate. If we contact our mutual employer, he would no doubt contact his own forces to bring to bear on the location. If we contact anyone, in fact, there is a good chance that Moriarty will hear of it long before we arrive, and like a rat from a sinking ship will make flight to the shadows of safer water. I suspect at least one of your workmen is in his employ and provided him invaluable knowledge of the site and the layout of the machines in the first place. No. We must at least ascertain whether or not the generators are, in fact, there at all. The time for authorities will come when there is evidence to give them."

"I'm going with you."

"Of course you are." Holmes looked amused. "I had already realized it would be futile to expect otherwise. Shall we go?"

The Lakeshore district was much as I could have guessed just from the associations one's mind may make to the words "warehouse" and "docks." A sort of sea-faring, seedy atmosphere that clouds over everything like thick pipe-smoke.

Buildings were two-storied blocks of cinderblock and darkness. It was nearly dusk, now, and I was feeling a weariness I hadn't allowed myself to feel in the last few days. When had I last eaten? My stomach gurgled. I faintly recalled there was a sandwich vendor I had bought a tuna-fish concoction from the night before, at the train station. Since then...it was a blur of events and revelations.

"The harbormaster of the near docks first." Holmes scanned everything with nervous energy. "I believe that would save us significant wandering. A quick inquiry of any nearby warehouses being privately purchased, but with no recorded deliveries in the last several days, should be sufficiently narrow parameters by which we can then search."

"But no deliveries would suggest it was an unused warehouse."

He crooked an eyebrow in what I was fast learning was almost a facial tic for him when he was delighting in exposing some observation to the blind. "Note that I referred to recorded deliveries, Mr. Tesla. Consider that a man like Moriarty and a plan such as this would necessitate as much undocumented action and payments as could be possible...and in a sense, that absence will be telling in itself. A recently-purchased warehouse that is immediately left, for all public intents and purposes, to lie empty and unused? A contradiction in likelihood. So a warehouse that has been purchased and then shows no outward signs of having been put to use? A good sign in our favor."

I remained outside the office while Holmes spoke with the authority. It seemed to be unspoken but clear that Holmes, though foreign as myself, was able to facilitate getting information more easily with his imposing height and clipped British bearing than my shorter, less imposing frame and Slavic accent.

I tried distracting myself counting the coins in my pocket, even making a slight game of transferring the larger denominations into another pocket of my waistcoat. Then trying to differentiate coins by their size and relative impressions. Even those minor exercises were insufficient to keep my eyes from wandering around me. After some minutes of nervously watching longshoremen enter and then shout their exits from a pub across from the office, I was relieved that Holmes came out with an agitated, excited air.

"Better fortunes than I should have expected." He chuckled. "The harbormaster had just such a number of warehouse locations available to report. No deliveries made, purchased within the last few months month through a private solicitor or incorporation, but no records given to the harbor authorities of any deliveries or shipments, nothing coming in or out. And despite my earlier reports, one solicitor used was indeed one of the three I already am familiar with as a servant of our man. These warehouses are located directly on the waterfront, just a few blocks from here. A majority of them are no doubt abandoned, just simply left idle or still waiting for their cargoes to arrive from overseas by way of the Lakes. But a search of these should uncover our desired hideaway while still saving us much fruitless hunting about the city. Come!" Without pause, he was already orienting on the nearest street intersection, headed towards the site.

We walked through five more intersections during our search. One of the addresses was quickly eliminated--it had burned down three weeks previous, and was a soot-and-smoke ruin of broken beams and dirty ash.

Hours went by with an unnerving speed. At midnight, halfway through our search, the area was still alive. Women of dubious distinction idled at the corners—one of them winked a lazy, drink-sodden eye at me as we passed. Large, broad-shouldered men, who made me intimately conscious of my thinner form, sang in broken, hoarse voices or argued with each other. Pubs were still alight with business; small hovels crammed in the alley spaces between larger, dark-windowed workhouses and warehouse storage.

Holmes moved as if oblivious to all, but I was sure he missed not a single person passing by. Each thing was no doubt identified and catalogued, every bar-counter song that reached his ears written on mental music sheets.

At the latest warehouse we arrived at, there definitely seemed to be something wrong just by its appearance. Unlike the others I'd seen on our search, this one's windows were boarded up, even those on the second story where the most ambitious thrill-seeker shouldn't have climbed.

And climb on what? There were no boxes, no barrels piled high, waiting for shipment. It was as bare a brick structure as to make it stand out against the street of dirty, packed buildings and discarded shipping-refuse. There were also less people in this short avenue that led off the main strip of the lakeshore road and towards the water. One sleeping figure, man or woman I couldn't tell, leaned against a dark lamp-post across from the front doors of our target.

"Approach with caution, but not *obvious* caution," Holmes whispered. "We don't want to seem as though we are about any unusual business here."

I nodded. We walked casually towards the front of the building. It was an inset double-door affair, with a two-foot arch of cover around it. As I followed, Holmes took us in a wide curve that seemed to go away from our building to the one next door.

He slowed to allow me to come alongside him. "We will approach by way of this far side, coming up via that alley between these structures." The shallowest of tilts of his head towards the figure leaning against the dark lamp-post. "I have suspicion that while our man is wont to work alone, he is not so fool as to not have left at least one watch-dog on call. Best we avoid being seen directly heading towards our goal."

In a few minutes we had gone around the neighbor building and carefully single-filed in the dim of the alley between it and the warehouse we were curious about.

As we approached it, Holmes pulled something out of his inner coat's breast pocket.

We stopped at the doors, Holmes leading. He pressed close to the door. He put his hand to the large padlock that was looped through two boltholes, each one set into one of the doors, locking them together securely.

Holmes twisted his hand. There was a clack-snap of breaking metal, and the padlock fell away, Holmes deftly catching it before it could ring on the concrete floor beneath our feet. Still, the lock's snap itself had seemed gunshot-loud to me in the quiet.

I frowned. Holmes held up the hand to me.

Between thumb and forefinger was a small, flat wedge of shiny steel. There was a hook-end to it, like a doctor's tool. Perhaps a dentist's item. A lock-pick.

"It never hurts to understand the techniques of the criminal, not just the motivations." Holmes grinned, pressing the right-side door to allow us entrance.

Inside, we encountered some sort of a managing office. Only twenty feet by twenty feet, it was windowless with high ceilings. I knew such areas from similar working arrangements I'd had before: walls quickly built with lathe and plaster to afford a small workspace away from the open volume of the rest of the warehouse. Light from the lone working street light outside fell through the door in a solid bar over our shoulders and into the room, casting monstrously thin silhouettes of us across the office. At the opposite wall from us was a door that should lead to the rest of the warehouse. I shut the door as quickly as I could manage while avoiding any slamming or excessive creaking.

As we stepped forward, halfway across the room, Holmes stopped, putting a hand to my chest to have me do the same. He leaned down, brusquely bringing a hand to the floor, sweeping it an inch, standing again.

"Staff." Holmes rubbed the gray-white powdery substance between his forefinger and thumb. He held it to me to look. "A better confirmation of our supposition, wouldn't you say?"

I nodded. Staff was the quickly-produced, plaster-of-Paris mixture that could make a fast-setting, durable wall substance that was being used in gigantic quantities to build the more elegantly decorated buildings of the Exposition. Shipped by train-car from New York, it could be mixed much like concrete, but was much more pliable. You could color it with certain dyes and shape it to look like marble, limestone, any number of different (but far more costly) materials.

I knew the slightly lime-laced acidic pungency of the material all too well. Anywhere you walked around the Exposition grounds would reveal workmen with shoulders coated with the white, crusted substance. Streaks of its powder even got on the sleeves of my coat and required a regular checking and patting of the fabric to beat it out.

The fact that the floor was dusted with a scattered piles of the substance, in a district where there should have been no reason to expect to find it, was a suggestion that someone had been at the Exposition site before coming to this particular warehouse. A suggestion Holmes had not missed.

"So this must be the place," I whispered. Eager to test this idea, I stepped around Holmes to proceed to far inner door.

"Wait—" Holmes reached after me.

Too late. My leg snagged against something in the dim — it felt like a thin, stretched wire placed at shin height.

I grunted as Holmes's hands slapped against my shoulder-blades. The force stung even through my jacket and shirt to my skin. I fairly flew to the floor a few feet forward, towards the door.

There was a click, immediately followed by the hissing, crashing rush of wood and refuse falling from a released catch-net that had been affixed to the high ceiling beams.

I landed, just past the radius of this collapse, skinning my right palm.

Holmes was swallowed by the fall of debris.

The wire I had tripped over had clearly been a trap, set to crush anyone intruding on the property.

I stood up, brushing off my hands, turning to look at the disastrous pile. It completely blocked my route back to the outer door. There was no way I could go for help.

I looked at the array of crushed boards and rotted barrels, bewildered. I could see no sign of the detective.

"Holmes?" I hissed.

No response.

Dear God, he'd been crushed! All of this, led up to the very door of the potential thieves' lair, and I'd stupidly blundered forward and—

I choked. Coughed on a bit of air-laden dust. My eyes sting with the smell of lime from the staff residue that had been blasted into the air from the crash. I wiped wet eyes with the sleeve of my jacket.

He had shoved me out of the way, realizing that if this was indeed his enemy's lair, there would of course be some sort of trap laid for hapless intruders...a trap cunningly laid that could be explained later as an unfortunate accident, all-too-common in warehouses with piled-high detritus and careless dock-hands...

I wanted to call out more loudly, but I knew that the noise alone would have already alerted anyone inside to my presence. Better that they might think the intruder crushed by their trap than still alive and approaching.

There was a whine emitting from the inner door. I hadn't been close enough to hear it before. A scratchy, rhythmic beat that one could just barely feel through the soles of the feet, in the boards of the floor. Coming undoubtedly from the other side of the door.

Machinery. Operating in a slow, churning motion.

Pulling my eyes away from the sight of the settling foothill of wreckage behind me, I went to the door.

It had not been locked. No doubt whoever laid the trap had been confident that there was no need to lock a door nobody would theoretically ever reach. I pressed the door open with slow care, listening for the beginnings of any squealing hinges that would reveal me.

I opened the door far enough to squeeze through. I could almost make out the echoes of my own breathing. I let the door close behind me, plunging me into almost absolute darkness.

Almost absolute...for there was light.

I was in a tiny, nervously-enclosing corridor. Whitewashed wood walls and an unlit ceiling of similar whitewash just half a head's distance above me. I stepped forward...onto a soft, springy substance, like a thick carpet of forest moss.

Rubber. I couldn't see it because it was dyed black. Industrial-grade, I knew it with the familiarity of one who'd walked on it for years in laboratories where electrical work required a non-conducting surface to walk on.

The corridor went on in one direction for roughly twenty more feet. Past that, I saw it was doorless, open to a space that was shadowed, but nonetheless the sounds grew louder, and there was a dim, sallow light flickering there. I hurried forward in silence, listening for any sounds of a floorboard creaking, or anything that might give away that I was being approached.

At the end of the corridor, the warehouse space was revealed. A huge, open space; I could not see its ceiling beams. Most of it was in darkness, but in the center of it were a ring of electric-powered lamps, eight-foot-tall stands with glowing wasp's nest bubbles of opaque blown glass that lent the space inside their circle a somewhat mystical, summer-time shine.

My generators were arrayed in two rows much as I had had them at the exhibit. Six in the back, seven in the front, with a cat's walk arrangement of steel grate just a foot above their cylindrical forms, where the oil reservoirs fed by natural gravity down into their catalytic burners, sending motive power into the internal pistons that then drove the core of the coil-laced dynamos. The storm-gray cylinders and brass-and-steel fittings shone in the light. They were bolted in place, and despite the relative weakness of the circle of lamps I could see they were running even if I hadn't been able to hear or feel their vibrations; there was the whirring of their internal works. Only the middle three were running—the others were silent.

As I saw this, a form appeared on the cat's walk above the left generator just outside those running. There was a scraping sound, combined with sharp clacks as the figure moved. That generator now began running, joining the first three. The reverberations increased in magnitude.

I stepped closer. I came to the edge of the lamp light circle, and got a better view of the man.

He was a hunchback. He lurched and moved within the lumbering confines of a massive black cloak draped about his shoulders, buttoned like a monk's cassock at the line of his abdomen down to his legs. He took steps in a loping, slow-but-lunging manner, each step like an act of throwing his entire weight forward to be just-short-of-falling by the intervention of his other leg, thrown forward to stop him.

He was older than I'd expected, or perhaps it was the salt-and-pepper of his hair and wild, caterpillar eyebrows. He wore nothing on his head, and his thinning hair was short, trimmed and then combed back with a center line along the scalp. His skin was waxy, pale, a nicotine yellow by the lamp-light. He was...perhaps in his forties? Early fifties? Nothing like I'd pictured. All that seemed truly telling in his posture and movements was that he was a taller man than presented, the hunch of his back and curve of his movement making him seem a more stunted fellow.

I had thought perhaps this man was truly the Devil, if someone like Holmes could react so strongly to his reputation. But this was just a dwarfish, misanthropic man. Clever, perhaps—I could see he was properly able to start the generators by means of their cat's walk switches, apparently not using a timing clock like I would. But not a Devil.

There was a gurgling hiss. The newly-started generator stopped, moaning with a bovine cry as it slowed, stopped.

Above, there was a spat curse from the man, and he lunge-stepped to the stairway. As he left the rubber padding of the cat's walk in favor of the iron steps of the stairway down to ground level, something new was added to his appearance. His steps, almost suicidally quick and uncoordinated in the tangles of his cloak and awkwardness, clanked like the striking of metal bars as he came down the dozen stairs. And a further discovery — from under the hem of his cloak, there was something that looked like a gigantic, banded snake, that followed along with him. He retraced its length as he came down the stairway, pulling it after him with a gritty scratching noise, like a man dragging a foot behind him, or a wooden leg. It trailed after him as he approached the down machine.

The generator was not primed properly. I could hear it in how it had suddenly failed. Like a man can recognize the pain of his lungs after he has run farther and harder than he can do so comfortably, I knew the generators as my own body. The fourth generator had been started with the gear-charge from the box on the cat's walk.

The way to properly start it was to let a trickle of electric current into its system from the prior started generator, so as to floodgate its energy at a slow rate. To start it 'cold,' using just the starter mechanism assigned to it individually, risked the generator losing sufficient charge to continue until it reached prime speed to generate its own motivational charge, and Moriarty had committed this same error. Now he was looking at the generator, muttering, scratching notes with a piece of charcoal right on the steel casing of the cylinder while he looked into its dynamo housing.

He was alone, then. Had he truly had any assistants, they would have been assigned to the starter-switch on the cat's walk, while someone else would use a clock or timing mechanism to call out cycles of the dynamo, and advise the assistant above when to level off with the lever on the switch, so as to cut back the starter's current in favor of that being opened up from the other generators. It was much like the running of an extremely complex and temperamental dam — part of the reason, in fact, that the contract Westinghouse next wanted from me was the completion of a power mechanism which would use the perpetual energy of water itself, installed at a convenient waterfall—hydraulic-electric power.

I stepped into the light.

"Professor Moriarty?"

The man whirled about to face me. Had I said he was not a Devil? I had been wrong. The Devil was now revealed as he turned, pivoting on one of his unseen feet to face me. There was anger, furious and not wavering like the lamps' light, but no surprise.

"I had thought my hunter's trap would have dealt with intruders to the premises." He smiled. "But I suppose even the occasional rodent will successfully get away from the spring-latch. What can I do for you, visitor?"

"You took something that belongs to me."

"Really?" The villain regarded the generators, following with a derisive glare at me. "From that accent of yours—Austrian? No. Serbic, obviously. I don't believe you're the industrialist. Which would mean you would have to be the famed Tesla, under Westinghouse's employ. You needn't worry, good sir. I'm sure your employer can afford to build a whole baker's dozen more of these with your help."

I pointed to the generators.

"I am the man who made those possible. And what you have stolen, I am here to see returned."

His smile was like that of a ghost-train clown, mirthless and wide.

"Come, then." He threw wide his arms. "Take back what you see as yours, by all means, my Croat friend."

His arms moving back tossed aside the dark cloak, revealing him in his entirety.

His body was the center of a massive metallic frame. What appeared to be copper coils were made into springs, corresponding to his forearms and upper arms.

Skillfully curved steel beams, barely an inch wide each, formed into a strange 'outer skeleton' that was joined to his shoulders, elbows, and wrists by flexible black bands—presumably the same laboratory-quality rubber I used myself in my shoe-soles and gloves.

At the shoulders, large ball sockets of metal overlapped his mortal ones, allowing him to swing his arms and the attached frame limbs moving in tandem with them.

At his chest, there was a series of thicker, brass-colored bands that went around his chest, ribs, and waist. There were metallic, flexible cables of alternating bands, rubber against brass, running along in a cross-grid to the bands, reaching out and terminating at the ends of the arms.

Each hand had a curled plate of copper curved over the back of the hand, and attached to these were foot-long rods of shining steel, each rod ending in a small, bulbous bulge just over the ridge of his knuckles. Underneath the frame, the mad professor wore what looked like a one-piece cloth suit, like a gymnast's suit, complete with gloves and sewn-shut feet at the ends of the pants legs. And where I saw glimmers of black and smeared shadow, the frame was oiled to facilitate its motion. The motion, as he waved aside his hands, made a squealing noise that reminded me of pistons, slowly grinding to prime a dynamo.

His lower half was more complex. It appeared that his legs, while whole, were useless. They had a wasted, thinner look than the rest of his bulk. The brass bands crossed his thighs and calves, with two massive bolt-looking discs of steel book-ending each knee to serve as a joint. Similar metal-and-rubber cables ran alongside the legs. Where his feet ended, there continued a large, elephantine 'foot,' four inches beyond his normal feet, of uniform, cylindrical steel, ending in 'caps' of black rubber, presumably to stabilize his steps.

From between his legs, revealed in silhouette against the dim of the generators and their occasional sparks, I saw a wrist-thick cable, more alternating metal-and-rubber.

The cable snaked away from him and towards the shadows between my generators. This was the 'banded snake' I'd noticed trailing after him everywhere.

The monster had made himself an outer-body like a loathsome, gigantic beetle. With the cloak thrown aside, he straightened and allowed his full height to emerge, a significant man who towered from the catwalk elevation over me. At my horrified look, his smile dropped.

"An enemy of mine cost me the use of my legs in a fall." He growled, casting a look down at his legs. "This frame was built to my specifications to complement my lost mobility. A wheeled device might have served better, but that is for another time, and more refinement. As it is..." The generators thrummed into their primary gear, sending up a shivering roar that shook the room, then leveled out to a snarling, chugging hum. "I think I have performed quite a miracle of modern engineering, wouldn't you agree?"

"What are you doing with my generators?"

"Doing? Simple enough. My endo-muscular, steel-alloy skeleton... or allow me some dramatics, my 'steel-o-skell' as I've taken to calling it...permits me to walk with short bursts of revivifying electricity to the proper acupunctural points in my muscles — a scientific delight I read of from the Far East some years ago, and applied when, bedridden in a private hideaway, I recovered from my ignominious fall. The frame not only delivers the shocks, but actually enhances the natural output they can produce, giving me a much stronger physique, as well as a measure of invulnerability to attack."

"Nonsense."

The monster's eyebrows rose, surprised.

"You could use a portable wheel-cart and an old junk device such as an Allis machine to provide the low voltage you describe. Why do you need my generators? They could power a city, much less your walking horror!"

"True." He nodded. "I could, indeed, do what you describe. In fact that is the very source of energy I used prior to coming upon your... gift. The generators do more than power my movement, now." He swept a hand in an awkward but grandiose gesture towards the expanse of whirling cylinders behind him. "They provide the power possible to soon protect me from any and all assailants, while I lead my various employees to reach the ends of my designs!"

"I don't see what your taking of my work will afford you."

"Oh, but you of all the people on earth could appreciate this power!" He practically cawed with a raven's pride in the telling. "Electrical energy of unbounded purity over vast distances...communication, much faster and with greater clarity than the base tap-tapping of a telegraph line! Offensive weapons that can be carried in a man's longcoat pocket yet release a force equal to any Zeus atop Olympus! Even electrical-magnetic charged fields that might imbue a chosen area with a repulsive protection ring as to make any historic legions of the Persians seem paltry in comparison, impenetrable to conventional mortar shell or rifle fire! Your energy generation, my good Tesla, is merely the acorn from which a larger tree of endless possibilities shall grow!"

The voice came from behind me.

"Thank you. That is all I needed to know to complete the puzzle."

Sherlock Holmes, dust sifting from his shoulders, stepped briskly from the darkness, whole and intact.

The villain had eyes like a pair of tiger's eye marbles. Colorful, but dark. First they were wide with astonishment, then slit as narrow as a knife's edge.

"*You.*" He chewed his lower lip. "I deduced as much from my spies' information. Only you would have come to such a clarion call as my actions on this side of the Atlantic. Like the attractions of equal magnetic ores, we find ourselves drawn together again, polar opposites nevertheless linked as chains in this life, do we not?"

"I wish it were otherwise." Holmes stepped around me. "You are sadly a discredit to the survival instinct."

"As I should say for you, sir," the creature retorted. "How did you manage to survive my little...distraction?"

"I cannot claim any ingenuity in that case." Holmes sounded rueful. He clapped his hands against his mantle, freeing up further dirt in light puffs. A small tear had damaged his right shoulder covering, showing the dim white linen shirt underneath. "Except perhaps that I was served by your own failure of foresight."

His other shirtsleeve was torn away at the elbow and I could see its length had been used as a make-shift tourniquet for that arm. The wrist still had the discoloration I'd noticed...but hello! It was half-gone now, and there were a few tell-tale smudges in orbit around it that said the markings were quite artificial. A ruse to make Holmes look as though he'd had chemical burns in the past.

His enemy's upper lip curled. "Oh?"

"Too many railroad ties and too much discarded beam-lumber. I was underneath a number of beams that fell in such a manner as to provide a small space under which I was fallen. It served as a crude but useful roof for me to gain leverage. The rest of the materials I managed to worm my way out of, once the actual deluge was completed. Had you more intelligently chosen stones, or cement-powder, I should easily have been crushed."

In any adventure story I had read, I would have expected a villain to laugh and stand revealed, proud for his infamy to be so confronted. Not so here. He stepped forward. Bold, long-striding steps that clicked and rang like tuning forks in the abominable machinery-suit he wore. Down he clatter-thumped the steps from the catwalk to the rubber-carpeted main floor, towards us.

He brought himself face to face with Holmes, as bold as any wolf that has learned the uselessness of the unguarded fence. Though Holmes was a tall man, as they drew close I could see that both were nearly nose to nose, even allowing for the inches added to the villain by his metal framework.

"I had hoped you dead," he growled into Holmes' face.

"As had I."

"You cost me everything I had, monster. Years worth of effort and strategy. Years of training and careful cultivation of my mind and reputation."

"The cost, then," Holmes brought himself within a breath of his enemy's face, "was a very cheap one, indeed."

The villain roared. A nonsensical and terrifying animal's cry. I didn't see what he did, Holmes was between he and I, but there was a sizzle, a smell of burnt air and ozone as his metal-framed arm swung in a wide, wild arc.

Holmes flew back into me, knocking us both to the ground. I felt my left hand go numb from the weight of the larger man as he landed atop me while we tumbled.

The lumbering brute loomed, a demon in brass and steel fittings, looking like a cross between a man and some kind of bridge, like the structural arcs that held up the glass ceilings of the Machineries Building at the Exposition. He smiled, hellish and baleful.

With a whir and grind, one of his legs came forward... the encased thing came down on Holmes's left hand, which had slapped on the floor beside him as he'd fallen back into me.

There was a throat-clenching crunch.

Holmes screamed with a bright, jarring clarity that cut through my thoughts as easy as diamond on glass. His enemy pulled back the telescoping limb.

Holmes sat up, raising the reddened and purpled hand. Two of the nails were already black. His eyes went up to Moriarty, and as I was scrambling to get to my feet, pulling on Holmes's elbow to try and help him as well, there was a chill that was palpable between them.

Whatever confrontation they'd had before, I saw, it was nothing compared to this. One or the other, the winner of this encounter would not leave with any doubts as to the fate of the loser.

Holmes bit his lower lip as he got up, holding the wounded hand out from his body, trying not to jar it and cause further pain. I saw that same washed, whitened look on his face that had been there previously. The front of his waistcoat had two half-dollar-sized burned holes smoking into their fabric.

"I...had not thought you capable of such sadism." Holmes flung the words at the polyphase-powered man.

"Sadism, dear enemy, is a product of wishing death without having the quality of mercy to grant its full kiss." The villain inclined his head. "Ah, but you are blushing more than you should, are you not?"

I looked again at Holmes, and saw that his nose had come off.

Amongst the small scratches and dirt about his features, his nose was dangling from a scrap of flesh, revealing a slightly thinner, less crooked nose underneath, clean of dirt or injury.

With a swipe of his hand he tore away the false nose, blinking at it before letting it drop to the floor. A few ragged edges around it revealed there was more to be discovered underneath what I now saw was an obvious disguise.

"And so the lies are at least turned 'round to the inevitable truth," the detective muttered. A weak smile shivered across his lips as he looked back at me. "My apologies for the deceptions involved, Mr. Tesla."

"Who are you?"

"Isn't it obvious, engineer?" sneered the electrified misanthrope before us.

I could only stare at the monster, astonished into stupidity.

"This is Professor James Moriarty, late of London and Reichenbach.

And masquerading—rather effectively I will grant—as my own self. Well," a sardonic tilt of the head, "until of course accident reveals his true visage."

I swallowed, coughed. "D-disguised as you?"

"Ah, my lack of publicity does no justice." A cackle as the madman stood back, raising his arms as if an actor about to bow to the applause of a cheering crowd. "Allow me to make my proper introduction, Mr. Tesla."

A creaking tilt of the abdomen into a mock bow.

"Mr. Sherlock Holmes. Former private detection consultant to Scotland Yard and sundry. Also late of London, but significantly changed from his own visits to the Reichenbach region."

****

I coughed again on the dust that had taken that opportunity to catch the back of my throat. Eyes watering, I wiped at them with rude cuffs of my wrists against the tender flesh. I stared in horror at the faux detective that had brought me here. To the lie that was revealed as the true Professor Moriarty.

"I commend you on a truly ambitious and brilliant disguise, Professor," Holmes fairly oozed as his eyes bulged with a madman's hot, hard glitter. A hiss of steam, a spark arced with a crack between the leads that supplied power at the shoulder ratchet-points to the arms. I slowly helped to grip my arm and accept the assistance. His body felt like immense dead weight, and his legs wouldn't accept his commands and re-assert themselves.

As he opened his eyes, I perceived that lighthouse inside him as burning brighter...oh but for the cold that emanated through his very look! "It seemed fitting," Moriarty *neé* Holmes answered dryly.

A bark that served Holmes' mutilated laughter, sharp as fine drill-heads in my ears. His vulture face darted forward, a beak nose that flared to take in the ozone-laden air around us.

"Fitting! To hear you speak of *fitting!*" He raised both hands up, bringing up those knob-ended brass-and copper contraption. "And to think, only a moment ago you spoke of my own depths of sadism!" A spitting sound. "Fitting should have been your death and my survival! Even so, it would have been tragic yet still an acceptable term to me, if the only option had been to have us both taken down into the foam of the falls, lost forever. Not to see my own features, my very name, abused in such a manner by the absolute worst candidate for its usurpation I could ever have imagined!"

He closed the arc further, until his upraised forearm made a small sandwich of space between those strange brass-plate balls attached to the forearm's girder-gauntlets, in turn wrapped 'round that wasted wound within.

"But that the true end should be you, hale and healthy and walking about while I was mangled and barely alive...that you should of all people impersonate me...!"

Arcs began to spark with swirls and bolts of brilliant, blue-white electricity. They flickered and groaned and sizzled between the two poles mounted to his arms. The whole thing suggested the unwelcome thought that it was an electrical garrote wire, about to strangle us with burning strength.

I was holding Moriarty by the elbow, helping to keep his balance, but the sparks transfixed the professor in place, like the tales of Indian snake charmers and their charges wavering, hypnotized.

"I am sorry, Holmes," he spoke with no motion in his features save for his lips, yet his voice broke on the utterance of the detective's name. "My agents found you and it was on my order alone that they took you from that place, cared for you, tried to raise you back to health...I found in myself a betrayal of my own being, that I could not so blithely, so coldly discard a mind and spirit as yours, even as you opposed my own...but you..."

The lantern face glowing in rage beamed down. "Yes! Even twisted, bereft of any ability to walk, I managed my escape from your jailers, and was able to make my way here!"

"Not jailers, my friend," Moriarty shook his head. As he did so, he reached up and tugged away at more of the masquerade, revealing a heavier-lined forehead...a chin that was differently angled, stronger yet had been made to look weak by an artful application of some sort of celluloid and rubber mixed, painted to look like skin, that changed the angle to something sharper and had given it the appearance of being narrower, longer. "They were physicians and specialists, the best I could procure to try and save what they could of you. When you escaped, we were easily able to track you, but...I ordered Colonel Moran to stand down. I ordered them all to stand down and take no action. The deeds were done, and I could no more take back what had happened to you than King Canute could command the waves to go back into the seas." His eyes were bright and sharp with a pain I could see had nothing to do with his crushed hand. "I had no idea that while we were perceiving only physical illness and injury that you had suffered...that more damage had been done within...and then I thought you dead when we lost the trail. Even in your condition, you artfully evaded my proxies."

"Your sympathy and your flattery can go to Perdition with the rest of you!" Holmes spat, and the electrical arc surged, thickened, ejected stray blue-white sparks that made the room smell of burning, of heavy stones being cut with blades and leaving that hard, acrid smell of torn earth and heaven in its wake. The generators were beginning to make a sound as a pack of metallic hounds, baying for the scent of the fox and this hellish master pointing them out the way.

Then the sparks intensified, seemed to shift their trajectories and float instead of simply falling away and dying out. Fairy flickers that made the air around the insane man look as though a line of delicate light bulbs had been strung about his shoulders and arms.

I recognized the phenomenon: the ionizing of air into a charge, passing the feed from my generators to his supercharged wireframe, out into the connection nodes that were the terminating ends of those rods.

Bring the rods together on the same contact surface...and the surface, and all that was part of it, completed the cycle of energy and allowed the power to curl through, finishing from one rod to the other.

If that conducting surface, though, were a human being...

I cast a glance at Moriarty. He was biting his lower lip. It was clear he was similarly frozen. He could do nothing but let those arcs glitter in the reflective wet of his eyes.

Holmes' arms coruscated with power. The generators, responding to the demand for more energy, were whining and beginning to smoke; huge thread-lengths of black that were snaking out from the large cylindrical housings behind him like the rising smoke of stacks in the factory districts. I could tell Holmes hadn't bothered to keep refreshing the oil in their pistons. The magnetos inside were getting hot from the friction.

The arcs of energy were spitting, hissing lengths of sporadic white light running along the villain's frame. They traveled up across his padded arms and out of the rods, forming a twisting, roiling coil of pure electricity.

That was when the man with the raised arms full of godly lightning, the heavens twisted into bright stripes of writhing fury and lighting his face with actinic agony, roared the word that made everything go horribly, utterly silent inside my mind for a heart's beat.

"No more, Moriarty! No more!"

I grabbed the professor by his shoulder, pulling his face to mine, an inch apart and smelling each other's sweat, the fear that galvanized our bones reeking off through our fine suits.

"Moriarty?" I yelled helplessly into his face.

Holmes hadn't oiled the pistons.

He knew the application of my technology, but like Westinghouse and Edison, didn't appreciate the care, the finesse, that the machinery demanded from its keepers. Perhaps with time he would've learned, being the man of intellect he was. But he'd had little time with them so far.

He couldn't appreciate the risk of what happened next.

As he lowered his arms, the light sputtering off him illuminated the box shape attached to the upper curve of the center generator's main dynamo housing. I saw a wisp of gray-black smoke come out of it.

Everything went into a slow, dreamy series of events that afterwards seemed inevitable.

The box shape, about four feet by three, was welded to the cylindrical housing. It was a thin-walled box, I knew from my own blueprints. We'd lost half a dozen of them in the construction of the generators when they'd been assembled at the Exposition.

I saw that this one had a hole gouged in it...probably by someone unfamiliar with such a device and assembling it only with respect to the parts fitting together, not by its own delicacy.

The box shape was my governor. The device that made certain the power the generators produced was forced into an even, modulated flow.

I let go of Moriarty. My hand mindlessly reached into my pocket.

The cold, hard iron nub of the acid-burnt bolt he'd tossed to me earlier met my fingers.

If I'd thought about it, I would have missed.

But instead, when I reared my arm back and witlessly flung the thing, the bolt went straight from pocket to hand, from hand to air, and met with the gap in the governor box with an explosive ringing noise.

There was a susurrus of squeals and groans in the dynamo, then the sound escalated. Faster, more furious. The generator was over-charging.

Holmes' face transformed from hateful triumph into an agonized scream that fell in timbre with the sound of the rising generator noise.

The arc of lightning that had been forming between his two hand-rods burst outwards like a soap-bubble, licking at the overhead beams and dissipating, leaving thick scorch-marks the length the path it had decayed along.

Holmes could make no sound. The generator had surged, and I could only guess what that meant for the energy coursing into his manufactured suit of armor.

His limbs began to shake, and I could hear loud scratching and popping noises, as if the air itself were being played over one of the new wax-cylinder phonograph-players. A smell of cooking rubber and noxious ozone plumed around me. I gasped, trying to breathe the smoky mixture. Moriarty was coughing beside me, hunched and wheezing.

The former detective's hair burst into flames. His eyes, the jittering tips of his darkening fingers...all of him fell victim to the electricity that I knew so well. She is a voltaic mistress, a galvanizing bride, but if driven to the prostitution of being coerced like so many draught-horses, she becomes a horrid Fury, amperages blazing. I could not describe in any useful detail the full, explosive power that had its way with the lost detective.

As it anchored him in place, I saw other flames shooting out of the joints of his suit, licking eagerly at the streaks of machine-oil coating his under-suit. There was a new smell—something sickly-sweet that I hope to never smell again, like simmering beef broth left too long on an oven's burner—and a vinegary, wine-dark scent underneath that...the smells of copper and tannic.

"No!"

I couldn't help it. I realized the true weight of it as Holmes' mouth popped with flame and something dark and smoking that might have been the remnants of his tongue. I ran past his molten form, towards my generators.

I blinked, trying to follow the sinewy line of the cable that had transmitted power from my machines to his body.

There. Ten feet inwards, in the back of the small alley made between the two central generators, the one on my left the damaged and shuddering one. A sort of larger version, and more crudely made, of my governor designs. I considered briefly that Holmes, for all his lost faculties, must have been a man of great intuitive ability. I ran forward.

He had used similar cables to break the relay! I could see that his 'governor,' instead of being a device for each generator, was in fact a single conduit station. There were cables leading off in many directions, all of them I saw leading to individual generators.

The damned fool! For all his brilliance, he'd been no appreciator of electricity whatsoever! He'd seen it like an early Greek saw hydraulics: a brute, water-current force.

Instead of my relay service, hooking the generators in series, he'd simply connected all their feeds to his conduit, then had it transmit to the suit on his body! Even had I not done what I had, I saw instantly that Holmes would not have had to wait long. His single conduit was handling the massive amounts of energy resultant from twelve polyphase, rampant alternating-current generators all acting independently, rather than reined into a controllable series!

What could he possibly have been using for a conductor? Even my purest-weld copper wiring in bundles hadn't shown such ability to carry such massive payloads of energy, for however brief a moment. Had Holmes figured out some method of fabricating a 'super'-conducting material?

As I contemplated this, there was a faint dish-breaking sound and I saw a scatter of white, pebbly shards fall away from one of the connecting leads at the central conduit. Like shiny chalk. Ceramic? Pottery? In a split second I lost the ability to make much more rational thoughts form.

I looked down where a brass circle-fitting held the primary cable to the block form of the conduit.

I leaned down, grasping the cable by one of the rubber ring-sections of its length, and jerked with strength I didn't know I'd had. I would feel the muscle strain of that effort even three days later.

There was a whine, a groan, a smell of more harshly-burning rubber, intense enough that if I'd eaten anything in the last few hours, I would have lost even that precious little.

The conduit station had been a feed-valve, as I'd guessed from looking at it. Like a gravity engine, if you removed the demand, the supply naturally shut down. Without its connection to the destroyed suit, the conduit was no longer demanding energy from my generators. I heard them ramping down, their dynamos falling still per my failsafe designs.

The damaged generator went silent, and a truly amazing mushroom-shaped burst of flames burped out from its central core, bringing a golden light to the entire chamber.

Looking around, panicked, I ran back to Moriarty.

I could see by the flames' light that there was an unblocked door, behind us, away from the ruin that had been an electric-suited blackguard. In the earlier dark it had been all but invisible, but now that I could see it, it looked like it led outside on the lakeside face of the warehouse.

"We have to get out!" I yelled into the professor's face. The smoke was thickening, the generator's heating metal beginning to screech behind us as the flames grew higher. We were only ten yards, no more than fifteen, from the nearest door and escape.

Moriarty stumbled alongside me, arm in arm, but as we reached the door, he stiffened, grasping my jacket lapel, dragging me to within inches of his grimed face.

"I have to see the body!" he screamed. *"I have to see it and know for sure this time! I have to see that he's* dead!"

He shoved me forward through the door. A hot, breathy roar of flame stroked across the threshold just as I collapsed through it to the outside.

I was leaning like a drunkard sailor against a pier support. The dank air of Lake Michigan swelled in my lungs.

Behind me, the warehouse burned, flames cackling, as if all the assorted minions of the Hell that awaits sinners were meeting for an All Hallow's Eve revel. The upper tiers of glass skylight had a magic-lantern show quality, oranges and yellow-umber glints like a mirror of the ocean with full moon fallen upon it, shifting and snarling.

I screamed, something that was useless and without syllables. My throat cried for water and rest.

A form came bursting out of the door, just as I heard the crank-siren wail of a fire truck, arriving on the scene on the street side of the warehouse.

Moriarty lumbered towards me, similarly falling to his knees and sucking in a long, tremulous breath. The bit of stage putty and makeup that had still clung to his face to give him the more thickened cheekbones of Sherlock Holmes was partly melted and had come free. He plucked the ruined gimmick off and exposed his own sharper-relieved skull, finally exposed as a completely different man than the one Westinghouse had introduced me to only the prior morning.

His face, soot-blackened, looked up at me with shining eyes.

"It's done, then."

The fire, though severe at the rear of the warehouse where Holmes and I had managed to escape, was put out by the timely arrival of the fire truck and its trained men. Their efforts were further aided by the fact that, in such close proximity to the lake shore area, there was a pervasive moisture that had permeated much of the building's more vulnerable wooden beams and lathing. They managed to still the flames before little more than a quarter of the building's shell had been severely blackened and damaged.

The damaged generator was a complete loss, but the remaining dozen were still in working order when I went in, handkerchief tied around my face to breathe, and gave them a casual examination. Only a few burnt-out connections needed repair, some polishing and buffing of the outer casings to get the soot and dust off them and they would be none the worse for their adventures. A dozen generators would still be sufficient for Westinghouse and the Exposition.

What was found next to the lost generator, in a burnt circle of its own cast-off ashes, was a shell that roughly resembled a steel-and-brass scarecrow. There was nothing remaining in that casing that suggested a human being had been in it.

When asked about the situation, I falsified a chronic, smoke-caused cough and hack from my throat. I waved away the question.

The police officer on the scene then turned to Moriarty, who was trying visibly not to touch or fidget with his wounded hand.

"What about all of this, then?" the officer said in an annoyed tone. He waved a hand at the blackened front of the warehouse. The firemen were already rolling and packing away their canvas hoses.

"Inside, Inspector—"

"That's Officer, my friend," the policeman interrupted. "Officer Delaney."

"Yes sir. My apologies. Officer Delaney, inside the warehouse you will discover thirteen generators that belong to Mr. George Westinghouse."

"The Westinghouse?"

"The same. This gentleman here," Moriarty nodded in my direction, "is Mr. Tesla, the inventor and engineer of those same generators. They were meant to be used in the upcoming World's Fair. They were stolen two days ago, and when Mr. Tesla and I discovered where they had been taken, the thief attempted to distract us by setting the generators on an explosive course. Mr. Tesla was able to deactivate them in time before they took out the entire neighborhood. I believe he will be most helpful in supervising with the removal of the devices from the property and restoring them to their proper home at the Exposition."

"And who would you be, then, Brit?" Delaney asked with sharp interest.

Moriarty hesitated.

"His name is Sherlock Holmes."

I was caught by a very real cough before I could speak further, Delaney's keen eyes watching and waiting for my remark. "From Scotland Yard. He was hired by Mr. Westinghouse to investigate and recover the generators."

Officer Delaney turned to me, dark hair slick and gold buttons over a thick barrel chest flickering with the light of the straggling flames that were dying around the corners of the warehouse facade.

"I thought you were too choked up to speak, sir."

"A moment's inconvenience. I'm feeling better."

"Can you corroborate this?"

I wanted to smile. But somehow my muscles, even those smallest ones in my face, didn't want to cooperate. It probably saved me from being arrested.

"Yes."

****

Moriarty was not taken to a hospital. Westinghouse arrived within the hour and had a private physician treat the wounds, in a closed room where prying eyes would not see to report any abnormality.

It took all the remaining time we had to have the technicians re-install the generators at the Electricities Building exhibit. During which time I didn't see or hear from Moriarty while he rested, presumably in a hotel room where Westinghouse could make certain he talked to no one in the newspapers. Westinghouse hired several Pinkertons to keep around-the-clock guard of the machines now that they were restored (I resisted the urge, with Herculean resolve, to remark about any 'too little, too late' sentiments in finally hiring a proper guard).

At late evening, a quarter past eight o' clock, May 1st of 1893, I swung the activating switch, and sent energy spiraling off into the millions of feet of wire and coil.

Lights surged with a moment's flare of illumination as the Allis generators were switched off in favor of the AC generators. Even Edison's tower of light had a short nova of power as everything began to be fed off my miracles.

Westinghouse beamed almost as brightly as the lights, making his speeches for the future of energy and America's brightness matching the wattage of the halos of light around the crowds.

As I stood behind him, making my polite nods and occasional clapping of hands, I saw a face glowing in the audience. A tall, thin face of an ascetic gentleman. He appeared to be giving a bored half-attention to the whole affair. The ascetic disdain broke, though, in the moments just before Westinghouse concluded the speech, as I saw him lift up his good hand and bite into something.

It looked like ice cream, but in some strange brown, bread-cone shape. He chewed on the bite thoughtfully before striding off and out of sight.

In the hours after Westinghouse stepped down and we began to mull about the exhibits with the first crowds, I received a note from a messenger boy in a corner away from the wandering multitude.

I left shortly after the second proceedings indoors dedicating the generators. I was going to be late for a more important appointment, according to the messenger boy's note.

The train station was noisy, busy with travelers, even for a train leaving so late in the evening. The 9:05 for New York was going to leave in a few minutes.

"Holmes?"

He stood at the platform, watching the other passengers load their bags, search for their tickets, complain to the conductor. He had the look of a man who is perpetually at a concert, one that only he could hear. Everything was music, no detail was extraneous to his senses, just overtures added to the greater work.

He turned at the sound of his name, smiling when he saw me. I was surprised to see the features of Sherlock Holmes back in place. Despite my awareness that it was all artifice and application, I could nevertheless not find any seam or edge to suggest what I knew was only a veneer of one man's face overtop another. Moriarty had restored all with seemingly no effort.

"I wanted to say good-bye to you," I spoke slowly so as not to trip my tongue on my own words. "I just...I can't thank you enough for your help in recovering my—" I almost said *life*, "—my work."

"Thanks are not needed, Mr. Tesla. It was a contract to fulfill. But guessing that you would want to do so regardless was why I had the note sent to fetch you."

"Are you sure you need to return to England right away?"

Moriarty reflected. Then he nodded.

"I have been gone long enough, I believe."

"Where...what was all of this?" I could think of no better way to phrase it, and had to presume upon his brilliant deduction to once again take its reflexive action in deciphering my confusion for me.

"This? Hm." A deep sigh that was oddly sadder than to me than the feeling I would have associated as a man is told his wife has passed in childbirth in the next room. Or the sound of a man who is committed to a lengthy prison sentence, one that will deprive him of so much even as the basics of survival will still be meagerly permitted him. "I should really return to my normal surroundings. I have a new home that I must make my old one. On Baker Street." A remarkably sun-bright smile brought a softening to Moriarty's otherwise stone face. "I should like to see the look on Watson's face when I return, whole and alive, to that rented room and all its furnishings. I shall be his personal Lazarus, and I have no doubts that many an hour of explanation will be required to satisfy his curiosity." A pause of reflection. "Perhaps I can trust Moran to accept an order of assassination...something to truly secure the illusion for everyone...hmmm..."

"But...why go back there? How is this to work? Surely you can't hope to fool people that knew Mr. Holmes so well!"

"It will be a challenge, and I'm sure it will often be a tiring one. I will especially have to take care where concerns the brother Mycroft." An arch of eyebrow as he momentarily considered this especially. "But I think any eccentricities I cannot adequately account for can be ultimately excused by these friends and family as the natural consequences of my 'surviving' and subsequent return. After all, such an experience as we shared...cannot help but change a man." This last was said with such infinite, slow misery that I was surprised to not see some sort of bright shine to the eyes, tears to correspond with such unblocked emotion.

"But why impersonate the man at all? Aren't you free now, to resume... to do what it is you once did before?"

Moriarty looked away from me. To the train, to the plumes of steam venting from auxiliary pistons. To the hollering conductors and cart boys soliciting to help with loading bags for a nickel or two.

"Have you ever heard the ancient saying," the stately man intoned in careful, measured notes, "that you must take pride in your enemy? That his victories mean he honors you with his challenges to be your equal, even your better? That even in death, there are many tribes in ancient land who honored the dead of their fallen nemesis at least as much, or more in some instances, than the bodies of their allies?" Another pause that was weighted with an invisible metal plumb-bob, swinging and wavering in its center.

He turned his lighthouse gaze back to me. "It is often far easier to look at the man who has died in battle against you than to try and honor with such pathetic things as funerals and parades the men whom you marched alongside into death, wouldn't you agree?"

"You intend..."

"I intend to honor the fallen dead, the fallen would-be conqueror who, in so courageously seeking to end me...ended himself instead. I would owe him no less. For my being alive and his...rendering to such pain and indignity before his end...would these not seem the perfect evidence, the logical prima facie that God and all sense of a moral order in the universe is nonsense? That nothing rules the planets and comets and the swing of a man's arm wielding a club against his fellow man but gravity, but physics and some coins in a pocket on a random chill night? Yet after...after we clashed that first time...I fell another way. A way I keep falling towards still. The notion that there is no natural morality...and yet morality exists nevertheless. And so who is its creator, its arbiter, the executor in the inheritance of the world from generation to generation? Why, we are. Each man and woman to a one. And where my enemy fell trying to enact that order...I feel humbled...obliged...to pick up the banner and do my pitiful best to walk the path."

"Will you..." I didn't know why I suddenly felt so hesitant, and I coughed to try to hide that pause. I don't think it fooled him for a moment, but he had the grace to not say anything in the space of breath. "Will you be safe, returning to home where your...gang still waits for you? And what of Holmes' friend? The doctor? Watson? You mentioned him. Won't he expose you?"

"Ah, well..." a very faint suggestion at the corner of the lips, as if a smile had contemplated making an appearance but chose instead to simply stand off-stage and watch from the rear curtains. "...if ego may be permitted... Sherlock was not the only man in the Isles capable of devilish-good deception. My skills in the mummery and the mimic of another man's speech, his look, his habits...I find myself looking forward to the challenge.

And what I fail to achieve in first performance, I no doubt will have many live rehearsals, shall we say, to get right in the end. Or simply attribute to my...my far-away misadventures." A faint twitch at the lips again, gone as quick as it had hinted at itself.

"But it seems too dangerous to—"

He raised a hand to cut me off.

"One cannot hide forever, Nikola." Moriarty said my name with the careful pronunciation of a man respectful of its original tongue. It brought a smile to my lips. I hadn't heard that sound in nearly eight years since coming to the New World. "Even danger knows the infirmity of time, if one is patient. My former agents here in America could be a hazard, but a minimal one. Without the head, the body quickly dies and decomposes. I have ever accepted that mortality is part and parcel of my chosen lifestyle."

Unprecedented, he put a light-fingered hand on my shoulder. I could tell that the motion was a costly one for him. He winced as he did so, the bandaged hand very unsteady on my shoulder.

"James Moriarty did indeed fall to his death at Reichenbach Falls. And Sherlock Holmes...well, I won't be so base or arrogant as to claim the best that was left of the man I knew...let us say a pale essence...survived. I must return, and I thank you for helping me settle an evil that I had foolishly thought marked clean."

His hand came from my shoulder, the bandage white against the rest of his drab appearance. His right hand began to dig into his endless depths of pockets and hiding-swatches in his longcoat.

"Ah." He smiled after several moments of searching, satisfied. He withdrew a curled clay pipe, yellowed at its bowl with long years of use. He clutched it in his teeth, nodding.

"Finally, I can have a proper smoke again." He used a deft and quick-handed match to light his tobacco, a fragrant cloud forming immediately about his shoulders like a second cloak's mantle. "Be seeing you, Mr. Tesla. Don't let your genius fall into such devil's hands again, if you can work to prevent it."

So with nothing further offered and no look back of goodbye, the great detective Sherlock Holmes—once known to the world as Professor James Moriarty and formerly the single most criminally brilliant mind in the known world, and who I would, sadly, never meet again—walked away without sound.

I've lost a lot of those kinds of battles, in the years since that evening at the train station platform.

And I am nearly for-certain, sitting here in my lonely hotel room, long-removed from those years and wonders, that Moriarty knew it that very moment he cautioned me. Though a man of his logical thinking would've scoffed at the idea of any sort of fortune-telling.

He could not have guessed that the Direct Current zealot Edison and others like him would turn my wonderful Alternating power to electric-chairs and destroyer-ship torpedoes. Beastly things that would have been what I'd expected of someone like the twisted Holmes, not the 'Father of the Light Bulb.' Or that some of my idle talks about death-ray machines and terrational stationary waves would be corrupted as serious ideas on my part, and make me into a scientific laughingstock in these, my finishing years.

But the Professor understood something about the inherent nature of all genius, all creative power. He knew that it is too easy for a clean, amoral idea of power and its application, knowledge and its curiosity towards the heavens, to be corrupted by a single man's greed or need for revenge.

He knew it all too well...and sometimes I've spent hours alone, sitting in rooms like this hotel room, and considered that his intimacy with that knowledge might have been less earned from dealing with Holmes...and more from the fight that he'd had to have had with himself, every day that he woke and looked at himself in the mirror.

The risk that power, as Byron said, corrupts; and the absolute power of a mind like that, could corrupt absolutely.

But of what, do these poets say, of the mind that has been corrupted...and by sheer will drags and pulls itself back to the light?

When I reach this question at this point in my thoughts, my mind can only go back to a single moment. As I said, I am usually not one to memorialize experiences as much as pure knowledge that I've gained in my time on earth.

And yet, the thought calls forth the feeling, the images and smells and sounds as I watched as he boarded the train bound for New York, which would then convey him back to his home in England by way of steamship.

I stood at the platform until the train's final car had become the pair of a dragon's red, lamp-lit eyes in the dark of night. I could not make my feet move, could not induce the electricity of my mind to activate my legs and make my escape, until the very last sign of its caboose train had curled down the tracks and out of sight to the Illinois plains.

"Pain is no evil/Unless it conquer us."

—Charles Kingsley
St. Maura

Ron Horsley is an artist/writer living in Columbus, Ohio.

He is the author of the "Everything Under" novels featuring the urban fantasy adventures of Body & Soul. He is also the author of "The World" series of illustrated children's novels and stories beginning with the critically-acclaimed *Beyond the Grass Ocean*. He is an MFA Graduate of the Columbus College of Art and Design as well as a 2002 Alumnus of the Clarion Workshop for Fantasy & SciFi Writing. In 2001 he debuted in the speculative fiction field editing and publishing the collection *The Midnighters Club: Tales from the Harker House Collection* and has had his fiction appear in numerous publications and anthologies.

For blog updates, fine arts & commercial design works, and news about upcoming projects, check out **RonHorsley.com**

To find out about "The World" series of children's novels, visit **BeyondTheGrassOcean.com**

For more about the "Everything Under" urban fantasy novels featuring the adventures of John Flicker's Body & Soul, visit **Everything-Under.net**

www.ingramcontent.com/pod-product-compliance
Lightning Source LLC
Chambersburg PA
CBHW020650130626
46552CB00003B/1476